GOODBYE TO THE OCEAN

GOODBYE TO THE OCEAN

Susan L. Lin

A Novella

Etchings Press
University of Indianapolis
Indianapolis, IN

This publication is made possible by funding provided by the Shaheen College of Arts and Sciences and the Department of English at the University of Indianapolis. Special thanks to the students who judged, edited, designed, and published this chapbook: Abby Bailey, Olivia Cameron, Desteni Guidry, and Liza Harris.

UNIVERSITY *of* INDIANAPOLIS

Published by Etchings Press
1400 E. Hanna Ave.
Indianapolis, Indiana 46227
All rights reserved

etchings.uindy.edu
www.uindy.edu/cas/english

Printed by IngramSpark

Published in the United States of America

26 25 24 23 22   1 2 3 4 5

ISBN 978-1-955521-05-5

Cover image by Chris F.
Cover design by Desteni Guidry
Interior design by Olivia Cameron

*For my parents
(and all their butterflies)*

0

"The wings of the Ulysses Butterfly are iridescent blue-green when fully open and extended." Those are the words he'll write twelve days from now, lounging in the passenger seat of his car with the windows rolled down. The weather report for that night: *Clear skies. Lows in the upper sixties.* Miles away from the city, you can see the stars.

"Her eyes are the exact color." Here, he will pause. Set down his pencil and shut the book he'll be writing in. "When she blinks, I see flashes of that same brilliance," he will say. "All the butterflies beating their wings and flying away." He'll toss the book in the glove compartment, run his fingers through his hair, and shift his body back behind the wheel. The key will turn in the ignition.

The sky is clear.
The lows are in the upper sixties.
A crescent moon lies on its back like a cradle in the trees.
My father will start driving back home.

In the delivery room, a nurse is filling out the form on my baby pillow, designed to read like a mock birth certificate. "Lyssa Wheeler." She says my name out loud as she writes it, stretching the *Y* like a long *E*. The sound bothers him, my father, who hears the first syllable pull—pulling, until it reaches the *V* of another word: leave, leaving.

He corrects her pronunciation. "It's short for Ulysses." He can tell she doesn't know what he means, doesn't really care. She starts slipping a pink case around the pillow. "Can we take the blue pillowcase, actually? The one with the train cars?" He points.

"Blue is for the boys." There is an edge of impatience in her voice, dotted with traces of fatigue. "Lyssa is a girl." Her eyes are set wide apart, strangely placed, as if they don't quite belong on such a young face. She has the look of someone who has seen too many beginnings and too many endings, not enough of whatever comes in between.

He still doesn't like the way she splits the name into two, that pair of syllables short and clipped. He doesn't like the landscape of her face, doesn't ever want to see it in my own. "Well, I mean, does it really matter?"

"Yes, it matters. We have a system here. The pillowcases match the baby blankets, which are blue for boys and pink for girls. See, these ones? They have cute little hearts on them—"

He doesn't really give a damn about the system. "Have you seen her eyes? She's named after the Ulysses Butterfly."

My father thinks I will do great things. He thinks my mother will find the perfect butterfly pattern at the fabric store and make a new pillowcase. He'll repaint the nursery to match. He thinks I'll have a little brother or sister in a couple of years. Our parents will raise us together and we'll be well-rounded and lighthearted and we'll go off to college and make them proud no matter what we do.

He shouldn't think about things that haven't happened yet.

His voice: *Have you seen her eyes?* I think I may be the only one who hasn't, yet.

The double doors open when we exit the maternity ward. I feel the air as it's pushed away around me, as it sweeps to the side in a perfect semi-circle. In that sound, I hear the next twenty-seven years fast-forwarded. Few things register in my mind; it all goes by too quickly, each individual sound—tennis shoes scraping the asphalt below the swingset, walking along a glass jar, falling off a hospital bed to the floor—crowded by the others, fighting for space. People around me are talking, their voices sped up. Squeaky. The hinges on that door need to be re-oiled.

Before we leave, someone takes my picture. I will find the photograph in fourteen years and see it for the first time. The first things I'll notice are my tiny arms, hands balled into fists and raised to my shoulders. My eyes are shut—sensitive to the overhead light—but I'll swear I can still see a hint of blue. A pink blanket is covering my body, the letters G-I-R-L resting on my chest. I am completely bald.

When they find his car later that month, it will be much too late.

Two hours away, a woman will lie awake, dreaming of a life she won't remember in the morning. She'll turn her head to the side and hear sirens as the fire trucks drive past outside. When she finally shuts her eyes, she'll fall asleep to the sound of her own breathing.

1

When they found his car early that morning, it was much too late. Years later, when I find photographs of his blue Impala—tucked away underneath her bed—I will try to picture it in flames.

In the local paper, his death is reduced to a few square inches of text. My father isn't even given a name. He is described as "a man in his mid-twenties." They don't mention the books. Maybe there was nothing left for them to find.

He leaves a surprise behind for my mother's next birthday, a silver butterfly pendant, the edges of its wings outlined in sapphires. She doesn't find it right away. After my father's death, she cannot bring herself to touch his belongings, instead leaving them where they were that morning when he left for work.

He might be sitting at his desk right now, reading that same newspaper with a new headline: **Man Found Dead in Mysterious Car Fire.** He always opened the metropolitan section last, scanning the photographs in the obits for children's faces. Sometimes when the elderly died, their families sent in an old childhood photo as a memory of the deceased's eternal youth. But most of the time, the photos were of children when they had died too young, when there weren't any other pictures to choose from.

"I know every death is tragic on some level, you know, for someone at least," my father would often say, "but it kills me every time, having to read these."

My mother had an easy answer for that. "Then don't." He would watch her as she came in and set a cup of coffee down on his desk, taking the paper away from him. "Come on, Art, you're going to be late."

"It's just—" and this one time, months before I was born, he didn't reach for the paper again like he usually did, "—you read these eulogies all the time, and after a while they just blur together in your memory. It's easy to forget that they're all different kids." He paused. She knew that he was looking at her pregnant belly, which was just beginning to show. Her own eyes were trained on his desk. He had a bad habit of leaving pens uncapped, losing the lids completely in a pile of papers, underneath the table, at the bottom of his bag. "Different kids," he repeated. "Different parents, different families."

"It won't happen to our baby," she said, reaching over his shoulder to recap a black pen. "If that's what you're worried about."

"Every parent thinks that." He turned in his chair and looked up at her face, placing both his hands on her stomach, like a protective wall around me. "How can you say it for sure?"

"Because." Her hands circled his wrists. "I won't let it. Okay?"

She can't see what isn't there yet—the two new ink pens he leaves, uncapped, on his desk that morning in the unforeseen future, where they bleed onto the pages of an open book. The spots grow larger and larger; one red and one blue until they meet in the middle and keep growing into each other, an ugly purple.

She can't see herself standing in front of her students in ninth grade English, letting the news spill out onto her desk, onto the papers she had to grade. They had seen photographs of him maybe, framed on her desk at school, but they'd never met him. They most definitely didn't know him. He was a complete stranger to them, and maybe that's why she felt she could let her guard down.

In the future, I'll wonder about that moment. I'll wonder whether it was a story someone told me, whether it happened to someone else I read about in the paper, whether it happened to anyone at all, or whether it was just another event in this Rubik's cube world I'd constructed: turning one set of actions in one direction, another set the opposite way, rearranging every face until I arrived at a pattern of colors I found attractive, knowing the ultimate goal was to match the squares to each other but never quite getting there. I'll wonder if any of the students in my mother's class walked out the door that day, changed in some way. The speech she gave was the kind thirteen- and fourteen-year-olds were often unaffected by; in normal circumstances, some may even have rolled their eyes.

"This morning, I stood in the kitchen staring at a plate of scrambled eggs and tomatoes and holding our baby to my chest, and I wondered if I should tell you what happened over the summer or just let it go. He was so young—talented, really talented. In many ways, his life was just beginning. Don't ever think that you'll have forever." Her hands hung awkwardly at her sides afterwards, not quite touching the fabric of her patterned skirt. The fingers of both hands were bent toward her palms in half-fists. A pause, and then: "Now, what are we doing today? Ah, yes." She creased open a copy of *The Iliad*. "I hope you all did your summer reading over the break."

Almost a year later, she's finally wiping down the bookshelves along the back wall of his study when she finds his gift: a small red box, hidden in a hole cut out of the center of an encyclopedia.

I sleep on my baby pillow at night. My head rests against those words, the ones that were written there on the day of my birth. It already seems like a lifetime ago:

This Certifies that <u>Lyssa Wheeler</u> was born to <u>Arthur and Rebecca Wheeler</u> at <u>Briggs Hospital</u> at <u>3:12 AM</u> on <u>Wednesday</u>, the <u>23rd</u> day of <u>May</u>. Weight at Birth: <u>6 pounds, 8 ounces.</u> Length: <u>19 inches</u>.
Attending Physician: <u>Dr. Brown.</u>

These are the earliest pieces of information that shape my life, at least according to some. They are the objective facts, the undeniable truths.

In fifteen years, a friend of mine will tell me that all vivid memories before age five are fabrications over time; they can't be real. AP Psychology. He's an overachiever, unlike me.

"It's not my fault you can't remember your own goddamn childhood."

I always counter unwelcome comments this way, even after I realize some people are offended by it. He is one of them. We won't stay friends for long.

I know this is real:
My mother sits at the kitchen table with her back to me. Green nightgown, hem gauzy right below her knees. From my place on the kitchen floor, I can feel the pattern etched into the linoleum—a series of diamond shapes connected to each other by perpendicular lines that reach from corner to corner, forming a grid across the whole room.

I see something fall, drops that reflect the light like liquid mirrors. Silence when they meet the floor. I prefer noise to quiet, in the form of wails. As I understand it later, my eyes disappear and skin wrinkles at the outer corners; my face flushes a deep pink. You can probably hear me three blocks away.

3

She wears the gift on a chain around her neck every day. Sometimes I wrap my arms around her, bury my face into her shoulder, just so I can touch the butterfly, feel it, cold against my cheek. Right now, the jewels press lightly into my flesh, just enough to leave an impression of wings on the side of my face. Years from now, I remember these moments the clearest—both the warmth and the cold—but I never remember letting go. And I will find comfort in that which brings me back to the past—like resting my head on a bare, icy shoulder.

Alone in front of the TV, I look at my reflection, see the butterfly, smile. A minute later, it is gone.

4

I learn to read in the corner of my father's study, the only room in the house that doesn't bake in the summer heat. His leather armchair is my new bed—I curl up with my head and feet on either armrest, a book open across my lap, and sound out each of the words.

Mom stands in the doorway, her hair pulled up in a messy bun. The ends stick out in all directions, framing her head. I think she looks like the Statue of Liberty, overlooking the New York Harbor.

"Art was the love of my life." Leaning against the doorjamb. "I gave my body to him. To it." Talking more to herself than to me.

My dad was twenty-six. She says he was brilliant, she says he was talented. Never says exactly what his talent was, but I don't ask. It could be anything, I think. A glance at his shelves is enough to overwhelm anyone. I can't read them yet, but he has books on every subject.

On the bottom, near the floor, he has a shelf for blank books. Sketchbooks. Notebooks. Some are written in—halfway, on random pages, in incomplete sentences. Mom gives me pens and crayons. I start on a fresh page, writing:

Hi. Bye. 1234

Scared of doors that won't open.

From the inside,
the knob is on the left hand side
and turns both clockwise and counterclockwise.

From the outside,
the knob is on the right hand side
and locks with a key that has too many teeth.

5 6 7 8 9 10 11 12 13 14 15 16 17 18 19 20 ...

In 18 years,
this room might be gone or lost or far away
and the books in it old and forgotten and never-been-reopened.

At this moment,
He is a 10 year old boy playing
flag football in the field behind an elementary school.

Lyssa
Lyssa W.
LYSSA WHEELER

He has a scar in the shape of a half-moon
on his lower stomach, an inch from his right hip bone.
I mean Michael Amherst.

abcdefghijklmnopq rst

If you're reading this,
don't forget his name that name that name.

uv wwwwxyz.

RED APPLE GREEN GRASS BLUE BUTTERFLY

Written just like that, except I misspell half the words and in eighteen years, if I pick it up, if I read it, it will just be a mass of scribbles and uncontrolled lettering. I'll barely be able to read a thing.

Mom is still standing there. I notice for the first time how pale her eyes are. In them are ghost ships passing each other on the ocean. For a moment, I imagine that she is not really there. I am seeing right through her, past her.

"Mommy." I blink. "You didn't make a noise."

"You looked busy, baby. Like you were writing something important. I didn't want to disturb you." Her whole face is shiny and white and old and young at the same time, with that look again, like she is remembering him.

She is frozen in the doorway.

7

In second grade, our desks are arranged in groups of four. The first week of class, we draw our self-portraits on white construction paper. I shake crayons onto my desk and start to line them up in a neat row.

"I need to use your purple," Alex Cleary says, five minutes before lunch. He reaches for it.

"Fine, but give it back." I start to put the other crayons back in the box. His eyes are on them as I do it. I give him a look. "What?"

"You have three of the same color."
Alex will be in my class every year from now until junior high. Every year, he'll borrow something from me—pencil, eraser, pencil and eraser—and never return it. He'll always be the sharpest kid in our class by far. I notice it right off: he notices everything. I learn to be careful around him.

"Three? I don't think so," I say, closing the box.

COMPOUND NOUNS EXERCISE

Instructions: Fill in the blanks with the compound noun that is created. Then write the definition of the new word below, using the old words. Print your answers neatly! Bonus: Write your own compound noun equation at the bottom of the page.

1. BED + ROOM = _bedroom_
the room in our house where my sleep bed is
2. PLAY + GROUND = _playground_
the ground behind the school where we play during recess
3. NIGHT + LIGHT = _nightlight_
a small light we plug in the wall at night so we can see in the dark
4. BOOK + ENDS = _bookends_
those things my dad put at the end of books so they won't fall over
5. HOUR + GLASS = _hourglass_
those glass bottles that are skinny in the middle where sand falls through until an hour passes, like in the Wizard of Oz

I write my own equation: BUTTER + FLY = _butterfly_ ...

"Mommy, why's it called a butterfly?" I find her in the kitchen, clipping coupons. She puts the scissors down, on the table. Her hand closes around the butterfly at the base of her throat. I don't realize till then that I've been pointing at it.

She thinks for a moment before lifting me onto her lap. "Well, Lyssa, that one's easy. You know how butter is soft, like ice cream? It's really easy to cut through with a knife. And when something goes well, without any problems, people say it was as smooth as butter. Just like a butterfly when it beats its wings—"

She doesn't finish the thought. Movement from outside the open window catches her eye and I turn my head to follow her gaze. A marigold-colored butterfly rests on the milkweed flowers, feeding on nectar. It opens and closes its wings, slowly, as if testing them before taking flight.

"Do you understand what I mean, Lys?" Mom laughs, her eyes crinkling at the corners.

I don't understand. In fact, I'm fairly sure that what she just said doesn't make any sense. But all I do is look at her and smile.

We also do a Butterfly Unit in science class this year, where we watch our own miniature caterpillars grow and transform into butterflies.

My teacher binds all our worksheets from the project together so that we'll have a booklet to take home, but I lose it like I lose everything. I'll never tell this story to anyone but Michael, only once, years from now and late at night. It comes out differently in words—not quite the version in our handmade booklets, not quite the version I carry in my head. He'll be sitting on the other side of the room, making his own book—not even facing me. Maybe he won't be listening.

8

Someone is stealing things in our homeroom. Mrs. Breyer warns us not to bring anything valuable to school. But she also says she knows the offender can't possibly be one of us.

Our school runs under an open classroom system, meaning there are no separate rooms, just one large space sectioned off with various strategically placed cabinets and coat racks. There are no walls separating second grade from third grade, third grade from fourth grade. Anyone from any of the other classes could have walked in.

"Of course it's one of us," I whisper when Mrs. Breyer is at the blackboard, chalking up our assignment. "She wants to believe it's not, but you know it is."

My friend Mallory laughs. "She thinks we're all angels."

When Mallory speaks, I can hear the extra vowels in her accent. What's your favourite colour?, she asked me on the first day of school, and I immediately saw the words form in my head the way she would write them.

But she isn't laughing anymore when her blue glow-in-the-dark pen goes missing. She had just won it two days earlier, when she guessed the closest number of gumballs in our weekly Estimation Jar Challenge. There was bubble solution inside the pen. She kept unscrewing the top off the end and blowing bubbles in my face. It was kind of annoying.

"Who do you think it is?" Mallory asks me this because I am

trustworthy, loyal, and perceptive. I know how to read people.

I pretend to think about this for a few seconds. "It's probably Alex Cleary. You know he's always taking my things, pretending they've been his all along when I ask him to give them back."

"But that's just small stuff, boring pencils and erasers. You can just buy more. I wish Mrs. Breyer would stop being so blind."

I don't think Mrs. Breyer actually believes it isn't one of us. I think she's trying to guilt-trip the thief into confessing. Somehow, I doubt it will work. Watching her closely, I wonder whom she suspects. She's a nice woman with honest eyes. I like having her for a teacher. Sometimes that makes things harder. Sometimes it doesn't.

I stop looking anyway.

The next week, all of the novelty pens Mrs. Breyer kept in the bottom drawer of her desk are gone.

10

The art room smells like poster paint and powdered hand-soap. Our teacher is a short, compact woman who likes to wear plum-colored suits. For an art teacher, she seems to have no imagination whatsoever.

We're making paper puppets of literary figures in class. We connect the arms and legs with brass brads so their joints pivot. Jennah and I decide to stage a battle with our respective characters: Odysseus versus the Mad Hatter from Alice's Adventures in Wonderland. Who will win? A decapitation (Odysseus'), a hole-punch wound to the chest (the Mad Hatter's), and four lost legs (everyone's) later, Mrs. Nichols finally tells us to "please stop, before someone gets hurt." Too late?

I won't meet Randy Byrne for another two years. The first time I see him—his back hunched over the drinking fountain outside seventh grade science—he'll already be too tall and angular, all jutting elbows and knees. His limbs are like the ancient banisters on the second-floor balcony in front of our school, impossibly long and skinny, uneven in their placement somehow. His eyes are a faded green, almost gray—the kind of color that comes in a box and makes a mark not quite solid when it meets another surface. They remind me of the sticks of chalk that teachers always keep at the blackboard. And this I may remember for the rest of my life: the oblong bead of water resting on his upper lip before his knuckles reach up and press it away.

He is the first person who will ever trust me with his body. A few years later, I'll really wish he hadn't. A mess of arms and legs and parts thrown at me—this time not made of paper, but skin, bones, organs, blood: life.

I go home after school and Dad's study is locked. My hand reaches for the doorknob, thinking for some reason that this time it won't turn. I don't know how I know. It has something to do with the temperature of the handle, which seems colder somehow. I try turning it to the left, then to the right again. Nothing.

"Those aren't all of his books, you know."

"Jesus, you scared me!" I jump back and turn around.

Mom comes into the room, watches me carefully. There were lots of others, apparently. Dad stored boxes and boxes of paperbacks in the trunk of his car. Often duplicates of his fa-vorites, so he would have them wherever he went. They were with him when he died. I will never figure out why she tells me this.

At night, I have nightmares: I see them burning.

13

These restrooms stretch across the back hallways, several times the length of one of our classrooms. There are only four of them in the entire building. In between classes, you can walk past and hear the stall doors opening and closing, metal latches clicking.

Two of them are girls' rooms. In the first: fourteen stalls, each door marked clearly with a number, one through fourteen. In the second: thirteen stalls, the doors labeled fifteen through twenty-seven. Some have deteriorated with age. By my last year of junior high, I know which stalls have no trashcans attached, which ones have the broken metal hooks on the inside, which ones to avoid. Once, a year ago, I was there alone after school, making up a chemistry lab. The lock was stuck when I tried to get back out, trapping me there for what seemed like forever. Finally I had to lie on my back and pull myself out, headfirst. Stall number seventeen. I ran home and threw all my clothes in the wash, vowing never to use that stall again, even if it's the only one open. I'll stand in line and wait by the bank of sinks.

A long strip of mirror looks over them.

"Why do you always do that?" Mallory is standing in front of the sink next to mine. A thin stick of lip balm, uncapped, dangles between two of her fingers as if she were about to smoke it like a cigarette.

"What?" I've always hated the lighting in the restroom. I don't know why I bother to stop and look into the mirror there to begin with; my skin always looks washed-out and pale, my freckles dull and sparse.

"That—" Mallory demonstrates with her free hand, "—cheek thing." She re-caps the stick and purses her lips in the mirror. "There's never anything there or anything."

Every time I see my reflection—it doesn't matter where, a mirror, the window, a doorknob—the first thing I do is run my fingertips down the side of my face lightly across my left cheek. One quick, fluid motion disguised as a nervous tic. I never noticed it myself before, but from now on, I become hyperaware of the action.

I feel the blood rushing to my ears before the color even shows and try to hide it by whipping my head to right, away from her, letting my hair fly in all directions before falling across my cheeks.

Someone exits one of the stalls up front. The door swings open with force, and I look in the mirror at the girl walking toward us.

The new girl's name was Melissa, but she wanted us to call her Lissa. I knew that was because they probably called her Smelly Mellie at her old school. I felt bad for her, obviously, but really, she could've used some deodorant.

Mallory and I cornered her in the bathroom one day between fifth and sixth period. "No one's going to call you Lissa," I told her. "There's no room for two Lyssas at this school, I don't care how you spell it."

"You can't tell me what I can and can't call myself."

"You think I can't? It's two against one right now. It could be three, four against one. You're the new girl remember?"

I watch out of the corner of my eye. The girl chooses a sink far away from us, methodically scrubbing her hands with the foam soap. Cold water is coming out of my faucet, and I cup my hands underneath the mouth so it pools in my palms. The door swings shut as the girl finally leaves.

Mallory is still looking my way. "It's nothing," I insist. She seems doubtful. "Really." I clear my throat. "Randy Byrne is looking even skinnier this year, don't you think?" I try to sound casual, raking my fingers through my hair.

My chemistry workbook from seventh grade science class was still in my locker yesterday when I cleaned it out, the Noble Gases on the Periodic Table colored the same chalky green as his eyes. Sometimes during free period, he plays Bloody Knuckles with the other guys. I think they're probably all idiots—he puts his fist down, knuckles to the table, and when someone shoots a nickel across, he pretends it doesn't hurt but when he thinks no one is looking, I see him bring his hand to his mouth and bite down. He wears elastic-waist pants and parts his hair in the middle and borrows my books but doesn't ever read them. I can tell when he returns them and responds to my basic "How'd you like it?" questions with the answer of someone who is only pretending.

"You know," I say to Mallory. "Randy David Byrne. Um. The one in our Algebra class." On the first day of class last year he told everyone he was Randy David Byrne, he always used his full name. From the start, he had an unexpected, fragile authority over people, whatever the reason, but now it seems to gradually slip away day by day. Again, whatever the reason.

I watch Mallory's reflection shake its head in the mirror at me before I bend down to splash my face, feeling the drops against my left cheek, like Mom's necklace all those years ago.

After homeroom I go back home, the perfect child. I do the dishes from breakfast, finish the rest of my homework—I even buy Mom a four-piece box of chocolates and only eat one. When she gets home from work, we start dinner together.

It's a routine we have. *Lyssa, baby, get those tomatoes out of the crisper for me,* she'll say, and then ask, *how was your exam today?* I usually say it was fine, because it usually was. I usually say, *where do you want the cutting board after I rinse it?* And then she replies, *bring it over here*, and, pointing to a spot next to her, *were there any questions you had trouble with?*

Today she starts slicing the vegetables, stopping midway to adjust the flame on the gas burners. She says, "Did you know your father liked his eggs scrambled with tomatoes?"

I have an answer prepared. "Nope, pretty sure I aced it. The whole thing was really—" I stop, realizing she just asked a completely different question than I'd thought, expected. "Um, the whole thing was really easy. I—"

Mom is looking down at her shirt in mild dismay. "Dammit, I always forget. Could you hand me my apron?" As she pulls it over her head and ties it at the back of her waist, I reach over and free her hair from the strap around her neck. She smiles faintly at me. "Thanks, Lyssa."

I can't help noticing she doesn't wear the necklace any-more, but I don't mention it. "Yeah, no problem," I say.

14

The day Randy Byrne tells me that he doesn't like seafood, "I don't really think"—in his exact words—is the same day I find the pictures from the day I was born, the newspaper article from two days after his death, the journal entries my father wrote when my mother was pregnant. They're in an old shoebox under her bed, crammed between a leaning tower of old, yellowed magazines and a ceramic pumpkin.

The newspaper clipping is in remarkable condition considering its age. I give it a cursory read, not sure what I'm expecting. There really is no mention of the books in his trunk. Maybe I'm the only one who even thinks this is important information. Maybe there never were any books in the first place. I never know when I should believe Mom's stories. Right now, I can hear her in the kitchen two rooms away, moving around mixing bowls and opening and closing cabinet doors.

The photographs in the box are glossy prints; instinctively, I pick them up by the edges, careful not to leave fingerprints, as if I have no right to be looking at them or handling them. I recognize Mom's handwriting on the backs. Some things have changed over time: the looseness of her writing, for example—today, her words seem tense, the letters closely spaced with no breathing room. I'm surprised by how straight she was able to write across in the absence of lines. Now her words tend to slope in one direction or the other as her hand travels to the other side of a page. I never thought that was something that could be lost; like the ability to ride a bicycle without the training wheels—it takes some practice but once you get the hang of it, you've got it for life. The revelation that she can no longer manage it anymore perplexes me. But the basic construction of her letters, I'm glad to see, remains exactly the same. I know Mom's handwriting better than I know my own, if only because I've studied it before, written fake notes of illness to excuse my absences in eighth grade and forged her signature. I don't pay attention to the way I form letters. I just write them and the way they come out is the way they come out.

A picture taken the night of his college graduation is lying at my feet. He's sitting behind the wheel of his car, the headlights on. I never knew my father's eyes were brown.

There are photographs under my bed, too: the mental snapshots I sometimes took when I was feeling blue, the snippets of my life that couldn't be found in any family album. The thoughts I directed towards her but never, never said out loud.

I always feel the ground under my feet when I first step into the kitchen: cool to the touch but like a pool of water on a hot summer day, unsteady. My toes hit the grooves in the linoleum and don't know what to do, where to place themselves next. Sometimes I think they expect a flat, smooth surface, not this maze of lines that I always followed only to reach another dead end: the back leg of a chair he bought when they first moved into the house sixteen years ago, then my left shoe, resting against it. I can't reconcile the two.

"Did you think I wouldn't find these." I hold up the pictures for her to see, but she doesn't turn around.

Light is coming through the window in what Mom used to call a suntangle, those rare spots of warmth that hit the ground in the distorted shape of glass panes, changing and shifting as afternoon turns to evening.

Over the years, scrubbing the floor has become a ritual: I only do it when she isn't home, once a week, when I fill a plastic bucket to the brim, water splashing out every time I re-soak the sponge. It's true that I favor cleanliness, that I'm wary of germs. But that's just an excuse. I want the floor to shine to the point where I can almost see my reflection in the surface: I like to look down on myself. That's a girl who has something to be ashamed of, I think, staring at the blurred features in the dampness. She thinks she has life figured out—she doesn't.

But there's also simply the sensation of being on my hands and knees, wearing an old T-shirt and shorts, making my way from one corner of the kitchen to another, crawling. My elbows slightly bent, my knees bent until I'm almost sitting on the back of my ankles. I see the lines on the floor as I used to—meeting each other somewhere in the distance. One of the first lessons you learn in third grade art class is how to create an illusion of one-point perspective. On sheets of newsprint, we drew street corners, power lines, train tracks, then watched them grow smaller and smaller, the lines meeting at the center and eventually disappearing.

I've always enjoyed watching a photograph when it falls, not that I've ever dropped one intentionally because I don't think I have. But when it happens—whether it's off the railing of a very tall ship, or off the kitchen table and into the trashcan, or something more innocent, like out of someone's hand when they've been holding it up too long—these pictures take on a hypnotic, almost ethereal quality. Like sheets of paper that nearly defy the laws of gravity because of their weightlessness, thinness, they cut across the air in curves, turning sometimes, twisting at various points of randomness. I wonder briefly if this is why people starve themselves. To feel light, free, flat: able to flip and bend in the air like that.

The picture lands in front of my feet, heads up, so I don't have to see her handwriting, just his face. The lines that form his shoulders and arms fall off the edge of the photograph and extend, strangely continuing along those lines on the floor with their forward-backward movement.

Forward—where the linoleum hits the wall, there is wallpaper, the edges of cabinets, a doorframe that leads outside, finally, away from this place. I'll be driving off in my own car, bought for next to nothing from a friend I never hear from again. I'll be living with Mallory, living with strangers, living with Mallory, living with Michael, living by myself. I'll be old before I know it.

Backward—I see landmarks, memories and the past, the lines carrying everything backward on their own now, the years flipping by until we are back at Dad's picture—back, even, to a time when this house had not yet existed.

My eyes follow the lines across the kitchen to the striped socks on Mom's feet, where I'm greeted by small squares of silence. Radium. Nitrogen. Dysprosium.

She's at the counter by the stove, baking chocolate chip cookies. Nevermind that they're my favorite, nevermind that they're probably for me.

"Why are you keeping these from me." My voice sounds flat when I phrase these questions; they don't sound like questions. I wish I could hear my voice, outside of this scene. On video, it never sounds like me.

"Lys, could we maybe not talk about this now?" Mom is talking to the batter, trying to shape it with her fingers. I don't know how she even knows what I'm referring to—she hasn't looked up since I entered.

She has the hands of a pianist, although she has never played as far as I know. Then again, there is a lot she never tells me. Those fingers are very long, thin, but decidedly strong. I remember how she placed them on my back when I was younger, bent over me when she thought I was already asleep but I could feel her breath on my neck and I smiled, ticklish, stifling my laughter. She probably thought I was dreaming.

There were the daily naps I took on her bed in the evenings while she was cooking dinner. I remember she always framed the bed with chairs to catch me if I fell. She was always over-protective, afraid I might somehow roll over three times in the same direction, right off the edge until I hit the floor.

But in those moments when she would wake me by shaking me lightly, I felt a sense of balance in the world—or at least my world—as if all those fingertips were pushing against flesh with the exact same amount of pressure, equidistance apart. It was as if she were molding my body and my life into something everyone would later call beautiful, removing those rough edges, the sharp corners, bad hair days, the asymmetry and imperfections in my bone structure that really did magically disappear: nightmares I would later have, given away like treats to kids with a plastic jack-o-lantern bucket on Halloween evening. They could handle them for one night.

And if my eyes opened to my mother, hovering over me, light spilling into the room through a crack between the curtains—light, and light's colors, the yellows and oranges, even those unexpected, reflected blues, finding her hair and nesting there—was that only a dream? Behind her shoulder, another figure and face up against the wall, wearing a glass mask, but still looking down at me. The face I now recognized, but the expression that came with it, not entirely. Was it one of pride or one of disappointment?

"Why did you tell me I had his eyes." The flatness is still there with us, in the kitchen with the blue sea floor, mimicking his photographs in all their two-dimensionality. I mean the photographs under the bed—the only tangible evidence, I think, of her hands on his body once upon a time. "His eyes. They're brown, not blue."

She's moving the balls of batter around on the cookie sheet as if they'll spell out an answer. "There's something you might not know about the Ulysses Butterfly—"

"I don't want to hear. About the Goddamn Ulysses Butterfly." The irony of this statement does not escape me, even at the moment. I'm the one with the encyclopedia entry, the square of paper that I look at constantly, if not to study the photograph and the words that attempt to illustrate and describe an elusive and faraway family of insects, then to marvel at the skill of the hands that had cut it out. All the corners are right angles, the lines straight. "I'm talking about my father's eyes."

"And I'm talking about the Ulysses Butterfly," she says. My identity is wrapped around the label and those words—the ones on the page and the ones in her mouth. She thinks she can tell me something I don't know about myself, but I don't know how that's possible.

The visual part of my brain is far quicker than the part that analyzes and explains; before I even start thinking about her response, I'm zipping through my mental collection of snapshots, backwards from this moment, all the thoughts I've had that I kept to myself. Some are minor things, others are more significant. It is hard to keep a blank face, especially when I can't see myself as she sees it right now—she has finally turned to look at me—but I avoid worrying about this by flipping through the photographs in my head at an even faster pace. As each one goes by, I feel more and more elated and light-headed, a sense of satisfaction rising within, thinking that I have surpassed her at her own game: I now have more secrets than she does.

Her eyes like a sea-haunt. I can see how grown men might get lost under them for ten years or more at a time, and never return home. It's a foggy place, one where lights find each other in clusters and give off a hazy glow, like a strange half-familiar world coming to greet you. I picture my father: red hair, brown eyes, blue shirt, arms that go on forever. *Time to head home*, he says. He takes a shortcut down a gravelly road when sudden waves cut across the side of his ship—water meeting earth, meeting fire.

I have no doubt that her eyes have paled even more with time. Something in them frightens me—I imagine them ten years from now, a shade of blue so light that it can only be perceived as white. No longer ghost ships in the ocean but a flat, two-dimensional drawing of them come ashore, dashing themselves upon the rocks, and then a white gleam: the lighthouse beam hitting a mirror.

Mom's hand reaches up to the back of her neck and stays there for a few seconds, fingers running across the knobs in her upper spine. She's feeling for the clasp of a necklace that is no longer there. I can't believe it. A year has passed. Is it possible she still forgets that it's gone, or is she trying to tell me something in her own, subtle way?

I start to speak again, faster and more loudly. "I don't even know what to say to you right now—I can't even think—what were you thinking—you know, you're the mother here—" My voice has taken on a strange tone, one that has a considerable number of bumps and dips, and I try to smooth them out but feel myself failing, feel myself falling, "—you're supposed to be handling this—I can't be expected to do it on my own—and you're keeping him all to yourself, why?—it's obvious now that you don't want to remarry—it's obvious I'll never have a real father—" I become aware that my arms are moving erratically in every direction. They are out of my control; their movements don't seem to match my words or my voice, sometimes sweeping downward during vocal bumps, upward at the dips.

The photographs start to escape my tenuous grip, one by one, flying to my left and right—some behind me. It is impossible to watch them all at once, but that doesn't stop me from trying. I twist my body in one direction and then the next, looking up and down, dimly aware of the absurdity but unable to stop. I wait for that familiar wave of peace to wash over me as I witness this rare beauty, but it never comes. Instead, I see all those eyes in the pictures, each one judging me, blaming me—first Mom's, then Dad's, then finally my own: those blue-green eyes from fourteen years ago, getting a glimpse at the future.

15

I sit on a plastic stool on the balcony outside Mallory's bedroom window and watch her smoke, trying not to look like I'm holding my breath.

"My dad's thinking about moving back to Australia," she says, tapping the end of her cigarette in an old plastic soap dish that now masquerades as an ashtray. Her family lived there, near the east coast of the island until she was seven. "I'll probably get to go back and visit this summer after school lets out." I actually hear her accent crawl back into certain pockets of her voice as she blows smoke out between her teeth.

"My parents went to Australia for their honeymoon," is all I say, staring over the railing at the street below. A group of little kids are kicking a soccer ball around; the lifeguard at the pool across the road blows his whistle.

"Really?" Mallory sounds surprised, but not entirely interested. "I never knew that. God, I love it there. I can't wait to go back." She leans her head back against the brick wall. "Hey." She taps me lightly on the arm. "You should come with, next chance I get to go back."

I don't know what to say to that—I don't dare hope it will actually happen. "Mmm." I make a noncommittal movement with my head, cover my mouth discreetly with one hand, and cough.

On my way home, I walk past Randy Byrne's house, even though I know he won't be home. Days before, I went to the front office at school to get all the paper work I needed for my driving permit. The state wants to make sure I'm enrolled in school, wants to make sure I have some sort of purpose in life, I guess. Goals. Alex Cleary, the boy from elementary school who always took my things, now works at the office desk for course credit. "We haven't had a class together since sixth grade," he said, a fact of which I was aware and for which I was also thankful. It wasn't because he stole from me—everything he took was unimportant or inconsequential in a larger sense, as Mallory had pointed out years ago. It was because he was too perceptive. It was because I always dozed off in the afternoons during our history lesson in that last class, and he would kick the leg of my chair trying to wake me. *Lyssa, Lyssa,* he whispered. In my sleep, I turned around to face him. *Lyssa, I know what you did in third grade. And I know the story behind your little trio of crayons the year before that. I know it, I know you. I know you!* When I jumped in my seat and woke up, he was still kicking. "Lyssa," he said, "Can I borrow your pencil? I promise I'll give it back."

A few days ago, in the office, he said, "Can you believe how many years have passed? Bet you're real excited to start driving." I wasn't really; I like walking. But I nodded at Alex, just to be agreeable. He'd grown up, it seemed, finally started using his gifted brain—in some ways, probably the sweetest boy I'd ever meet. I still hoped I'd never see him again.

Randy lives in a neighborhood where everyone has perfectly manicured lawns, where people next door always seem to be looking over the fence at you, shaking their heads, saying: *no, don't do that, don't do what you're thinking, I'm watching you.* The Byrnes have a two-story house with salt-and-pepper-colored bricks. The window on the second floor, far left, is the one that opens to Randy's room. His couldn't be more different from Mallory's. Her walls are painted in blue and violet stripes, her name spelled out on the wall in playful white letters attached with magnets to a metal strip. Every time I'm there, I rearrange the letters to spell something different: RALLY. LYRA. ROMA. ALL OR MY. AMORY.

The walls in Randy's room are eggshell white and mostly plain. When he was eight, his father nailed a gigantic poster of the Periodic Table onto his back wall where most parents might nail a map of the world. By the time he was nine, Randy had memorized all the elements, their symbols, and their atomic numbers. I was the one who started spelling his name RaNDy: Radium Nitrogen Dysprosium. Randy David Byrne.

One night in his room, I stared at the walls too long. Randy was in the bathroom running the water in the tub, and I was starting to see something familiar take form in those letters and abbreviations that once meant little to me. Downstairs, it was quiet. His parents never seemed to be home. I couldn't even say why. I knew his father spent most of his time in a lab and worked long hours doing scientific research at the local state university, but I never knew what kind of research exactly. This was not the type of information Randy ever volunteered. And as time passes, he seems to say less and less.

I leave the neighborhood as the wind picks up and I wrap my coat tighter around my body. The trees are losing their leaves and some of them fall onto my shoulders and catch there, won't let go.

Back home, secrets collect underneath my bed the way dust might if I didn't clean. They settle over the floorboards like a blanket, thick enough for me to run my index finger through it, drawing a path from one point of my life to the next.

My best friend and I had matching backpacks in kindergarten. They were designed in the same style, hers with the characters of *The Wizard of Oz* on the front pocket, mine with Ariel from *The Little Mermaid*. For some reason, her backpack is the one I find when I hike up the bedskirt and look underneath. The purple PVC has a goldenrod trim and the words "Follow the yellow brick road!" written along the top opening.

Unzip the bag and the contents could swallow a room:

- *A half-used bottle of pearly blue nail polish.* No idea where that one is from. I shake the bottle like I always do to hear the tiny silver balls clink against the glass. Dried. Oh well. I toss it aside. My arm jerks a little and I throw it too far—the bottle slides across my bedspread and over the edge.

- *A nightlight with a stained glass butterfly covering the bulb.* I pick it up too quickly and cut myself on a chipped corner. This one I remember, I think, touching a tissue to the cut. Cody Singleton's, seventh grade. I found it in his room. "It ain't mine, I swear," he kept saying. "I don't need no light to sleep at night. It's my little sister's." I didn't really give a damn whose it was. It was in his room. I said, "Your grammar sucks, you know that right?" Now I set the butterfly down on the bed and watch the sunlight hit the glass from the outside. The colors! They fall onto my hands, dyeing geometry on my skin.

- *An assortment of writing instruments*: two ten-color pens with cerulean plastic bears on the ends, one blue pen shaped like a folded up umbrella, six blue, green, and pink push pencils, one pen with miniature dice inside a clear plastic tube, two pens shaped like miniature red swords, three sparkly crayons, all the same shade of blue. Christ, there are so many. I spread them all out in front of me, arranging them by color, then by age. My fingers start to feel numb as I wrap them around one of the crayons, my grip slipping over the textured paper covering. I open the mouth of the bag and see what's next,

- *A blue glow-in-the-dark pen.* Mallory's, third grade. She still doesn't know. Guilt bubbles to the surface, through the hole of a wand. I push it back out to the other side. I'll feel it again when I room with Mallory during her first year of college, but I can rationalize it away, I always do. It's not like I ever take anything from her again anyway.

- *A silver butterfly pendant, outlined in sapphires.* This one is wrapped in three layers of tissues and kept inside an old chocolate tin. I see my blurred reflection in the lid but can't make out any features. My whole body is shaking and I don't know why. I fold the tissues back over and stuff it at the bottom of the bag, everything else on top.

Minutes later, I remember the nail polish on the floor and reach over on my stomach to pick it up. My legs stretch out from under me, my feet pointed. The first time I ever see someone die, the hospital speakers will be playing Christmas carols, a glass of eggnog on the table next to me. I'll remember looking down at my feet, pointing and flexing them, making sure I'm still in control of my body.

Right now, I don't think I am: when I try to lie perfectly still, my teeth jump around in my mouth like bones trapped in an unwanted casket.

17

The sushi restaurant downtown won't hire me as a waitress because I don't look Japanese. What gave me away? Was it the red hair, the freckles, the turquoise eyes? I may not have dark hair or bone-white skin, but I know more about the food than a lot of the Asian-American girls in my class. Some of them don't even know how to use chopsticks.

I like to come here on Tuesday afternoons when it's not so busy and sit next to the back wall where they hang all the paintings by local artists. The only time I ever brought Randy here for lunch, he ordered a bowl of miso soup but politely refused to try anything from my plate. "I don't really think I like seafood, thanks," he said with a tight-lipped smile. His mouth turned up at the edges oddly; he wouldn't stop blinking. "So what's your excuse the rest of the time?" I asked, but the restaurant seemed to get louder then—people pushed their empty bowls away, stirred the straws in their drinks, and shifted in their seats, laughing at their own stories. I don't think he could hear my question.

"Are you ready to order?" One of the younger waitresses, a tall, willowy girl named Misha, is standing next to my table with a pad of paper in hand, pencil poised.

I point to couple items on the menu that I often order and one I have never tried.

"Good choice." She takes my menu and gives me a reluctant smile. "I'm sorry Lyssa, about the job, you know, earlier. It's restaurant policy. I've tried to get my uncle to change his mind—"

"No." I take a sip of my iced water and swallow. "No, you don't have to explain. I understand."

When she's gone, I look more closely at the wall beside me. There's a new painting for sale, a large one. It's black and white, a close-up view of a butterfly in flight, spanning the length of the canvas, its wings expansive. The painting expensive. When I find out how much it's selling for, I have the sudden urge to just walk off with it, but I don't do that anymore. Besides, it's too big.

"Who's the artist?" I ask instead, when Misha returns with the appetizers.

Michael Amherst. I remember the name.

I recognize some part of it in my memory. Is it a car on its way home, a poem scribbled in a notebook, a photograph of a figure from the past (or maybe from the future)? Sometimes I think it doesn't really matter anymore. *Hold on*, I think, *you are almost there.*

It'll be fall in two months, back-to-school season. This year should be college, but I guess I'm not going. All the catalogs they mailed me are buried somewhere on my closet floor, most of them still sealed in their envelopes. I never filled out any applications.

Randy—of course he'd applied, of course he'd even been accepted into a prestigious university on the other side of the country, but of course now he'd never go.

His body never seemed to be the right temperature. Some days it had been too cold, other days too hot. I always shrank away from the heat, like his bare skin was something I was afraid of, or unprepared for. It gave off a kind of warmth I didn't associate with comfort, or with love. Instead, it was the kind of warmth that reminded me of a sickness, a feverish need or desire or wanting that never yielded the intended results. It was easier to let go of the responsibility and look at the table of elements on his wall. I didn't have to stare for too long before I convinced myself it was just squares, a grid, my kitchen floor. I'd imagine climbing the walls, crawling over it, turning this reality on its axis—that wall easily became the floor, another wall the ceiling, the laws of gravity altered and forgotten until this room became another place altogether.

At the same time, I still coveted the cold, my cheek resting on his shoulder. My fingers could feel each individual bone of his ribcage underneath his shirt. I pressed down on them, played them like the keys of an imaginary accordion. Something wasn't right.

"Are you sure everything's okay?" I'd asked one night when he was being particularly unresponsive.

"Of course it is."

That was the answer I wanted to hear.

18

I won't last long as an art model where I am stretched thin all the time and not allowed to move—I go to classes in old clothing that can be easily removed and peel off layer after layer—this year after that year—the past falling off of me one year at a time and in the winter it's still too cold—even with a personal heater—even for me—the door is cracked for ventilation with absolutely nothing to cover me—and I wonder if this is revealing if this is the whole world seeing me or if this is nothing at all—if this is what Mom meant about giving her body to Art or if that was something else entirely—and the instructor tells his students to pretend—I am just a bowl of fruit—that's it—but everybody is staring and distorting my body on paper where it will stay long after I leave—because doing a contour line drawing means not picking up your magic marker before you finish—but doing it blind means learning to watch the subject not your paper—and in the end this is my life this is a line that goes from one point to the other this is one continuous line with no breaks in the middle—if you need to pause, yes, please pause, but make it quick, or the ink will start bleeding spots in the middle. Of the line. First time I remember doing this the roles were reversed—I was sketching Kyle Turner in fifth grade—he saw it afterwards and said "You can't draw worth crap"—the right eye was lopsided and his mouth was eating his nose—I said "it's not my fault you look like that" and that was that.

19

The night starts like all others seem to—someone says something about me that I don't like and I throw it back at them.

Stop making generalizations, I want to say but don't. I try to laugh instead but come up short. My trachea tightens, makes a sound like someone being strangled. Someone, not me.

Nights like this I feel myself flatten to the floor, like construction paper glued to Bristol board, a bookend being pulled away from either side of me. Am I just everyone else's collection of body part cutouts, mismatched and held together with brass brads—I'll only move when you want me to?

At Mallory's place, my mom leaves messages on the machine: *Baby, I miss you.* I haven't even spoken to her since I left home after high school graduation to move in with Mallory. "It's only an hour away. I'll come visit," I'd said, knowing what I couldn't leave behind would fit in a recycled chocolate tin and a pillowcase with a train running across it. On the recording, her voice sounds like an unfinished jigsaw. Her words are incomplete, almost like they're missing their vowels, almost like I'm standing on one side of the railroad tracks, only able to catch glimpses of the world on the other side as they appear, filtered through those brief spaces of light between moving train cars.

I m—ss y—. C—ll m— b—kkk.

When I see a blue Chevy Impala speeding down the free-way, it turns into a bed rolling down the hospital hall. My father is lying down on it, connected to half a dozen feeding tubes—he's smaller somehow, younger, thinner than I remember. I can see his bones sticking out in strange places.

I wake up not knowing where I am, lying next to a head, connected to a body, the taste in my mouth like I don't know what, pretending I don't remember anything. I roll away, un-tangle myself from habit just so I can fall into it again some other night.

On my way home, I stumble over the word—H-O-M-E—wondering where it is. Lift my foot to look under my shoe—no, not there—for some reason I think this is hilarious and laugh so hard I start to cry.

Everyone I pass on the street starts looking like a stranger with familiar eyes. I see them all pale blue, *something* recogniz-able on their faces: concern maybe, disgust more likely. There's a bum standing next to an intersection a few blocks away from Mallory's apartment, wearing a red knit sweater with a gigantic likeness of Santa's jolly face emblazoned on the front. It's the middle of April. The glow from street lamps, blue reflectors on the road, the red-yellow-green pattern of traffic signals, all join together to become oversized strings of Christmas lights deco-rating the city.

"Please, can you spare change?" the man on the corner

says. He's carrying a cardboard sign with the word *HUNGRY* scrawled on it in all caps. I shake my head, *no*, Santa glaring at me through his woven eyes.

I have to swallow as it gets later, earlier—what time is it?—to keep myself from hurling, losing more.

20

The encyclopedia cutout I stole from his study fifteen years ago stays with me. I can picture him with a cutting mat on his desk, running an X-acto along his T-square and straightedge. He was left-handed. A phrase in the article is circled, in the sentence that mentions the butterfly's "bright blue-green wings." In the margins, he has written, "This description doesn't do it justice," in an ink pen. The side of his hand has left a trail of light blue smudges down the side of the glossy page.

ULYSSES BUTTERFLY |yōō'lisēz 'bətər,flī|

FEATURES
The Ulysses Butterfly is characterized and easily recognized by its bright blue-green wings. However, it is visible only in sudden, blue flashes as it flies high above the trees, making it hard for predators to capture. When resting on a flower with its wings closed, the butterfly appears a dull brown, blending easily into the surroundings. It is also often difficult to photograph because its colors change in varying light.

STATUS
The Ulysses Butterfly is found along the northeast coast of Australia. In the past, sightings were so rare

that the butterfly was listed as endangered. The problem has since been rectified with larval food plantings
in the suburbs of Queensland, but the Ulysses Butterfly remains protected in an effort to control the number of these butterflies that are being collected.

The males of this species are often attracted to iride-
cent blue objects as the objects are mistaken for fe-
males.

21

Every first Wednesday of the month, I go to the local community college where they hold life-drawing classes that are open to the public. Eight dollars to get in, two dollars for an easel, light refreshments free of charge. I help myself to cheese cubes and strawberries and find a corner by the windows where I can sit and not be interrupted by the people who will sometimes come up to me: "You look familiar, don't you? Weren't you one of the models once?"

It would sound like a bad pick-up line if it weren't true.

Something about him immediately reminds me of a photograph I once saw. He wears clothes in faded colors and has a haircut that seems like it could be two decades old but somehow doesn't seem out of place today. His features are actually somewhat similar to those of the first boy—the one who trusted me with his life while I shrugged the responsibility off my shoulders, not knowing all the answers as I once thought I did—but this one is different. His eyes are brown instead of green, his hair a few shades darker than strawberry blond. I simultaneously love and despise him before he even introduces himself and tells me his name.

For some reason I hear the sounds before he even makes them. "Michael Amherst. Nice to meet you." *And he speaks*, I think. He's younger than I'd expected, only six years older than me.

Later, I'll admit I've seen his work at a local Japanese restaurant that closed down the year before.

"Yeah, I was sad to hear about that, when they announced they were going out of business? I ate there all the time." *He eats,* I think.

"Really?" This was news to me. "I don't think I ever saw you there. I'm pretty sure. I would've noticed."

In truth, he was the kind of redhead you didn't always notice in a crowd, if such a thing exists. Maybe it was the way those strands looked more dirty blond than copper in the wrong kind of light. Maybe it was the way his features were dull and unimpressive at first glance. If he hadn't turned his face at just the right angle, held his arms out in the vague shape of an echo, as if he were inviting something in, holding all the pieces of the world together—I might never have seen him.

I visit his studio for the first time a couple months later, and things start to make sense, or at least feel like they do. He has shelves along every wall, books on every subject. I find a notebook there, filled with a child's illegible handwriting.

When I get back to Mallory's, I look in the top drawer of the nightstand for my necklace but can't find it. She walks in my bedroom while I'm flipping through all the compartments in my closet, searching. "Mal, have you seen my necklace? It's got a pin attached, with sapphires along the edge of a butterfly..."

From the doorway, Mallory says, "A butterfly? Lyssa, I don't think I know about anything like that..." but she sounds as if she does. When I turn around to face her, she's grinning.

"Mallory! It's not funny, where the fuck is it?"

"Chill out." She dangles it in front of me. "I borrowed it. I was just about to return it, actually."

"This," I say, taking the necklace away from her, "is not for you to borrow. Okay?" I struggle to open the clasp and fasten the chain around my neck.

Mallory watches, her face expressionless. "Didn't your mom wear one just like that when we were kids? She did, didn't she? I always thought it was beautiful."

I close my fist around the butterfly and look up at her. "It's the same one. She gave it to me."

If she suspects that to be anything other than the truth, her face doesn't show it. "She called again today. Don't you think you should talk to her? Just so she knows you're okay? She sounds worried sick."

I don't answer. I'm distracted by one of the mental photographs in my head, the one of Mallory. It's changing. She's no longer that eight-year-old girl, fiercely loyal to me, oblivious to any betrayal. I used to feel safe around her, like maybe she didn't notice things. I think she does now, or at the very least she's starting to. It won't be long.

"Hey, you are okay, right?" She looks concerned. "Everything's good?"

"Of course it is."

Of course it is. Doesn't that sound familiar.

A lot of people tend to think of paintings as two-dimensional, but they aren't really. Not the ones we're drawn to, not the ones we want to reach out and touch. *A book is the same way. It's not just collected sheets of paper, bound together with an endless stream of printed words, you know? It's a 3-D object.* This is also Michael's explanation for scraping oils onto his canvases thick and dry, straight out of the tube, to create texture. *What's the point of a painting if it's just going to be some pretty picture on display? That's one-sided. You're not making a connection with your audience.*

He doesn't like the way museums feel, a labyrinth of white walls and silence, the yellow tape on the floor warning you not to cross. I don't like the way he drives too fast down unfamiliar roads and lights cigarettes inside his bedroom without even opening the window.

23

Scene: *A room with glass panels on one side and a door. Shelves of books cover the back and sidewalls. In the foreground, a girl in her early- to mid-twenties sits in a leather armchair. In her lap is an open book. She is lit softly by a light from above. To the back right corner of the room, a redheaded man hunched over a desk, working with great concentration. He is a shape in the darkness.*

GIRL IN ARMCHAIR

I love this room. I always have, I loved its sound, I loved its voice, and when other kids were tripping each other on the playground, I was watching words spill out its throat. Mom told me stories here, she told them standing at the doorway, right outside, when I was sleeping. At school, I crawled all over the furniture: I couldn't sit still. It was like I had too many legs— they were always moving, always propelling me forward and forward, but then back again. To the side. Forward. (*Breath.*) I always felt like I had too many legs.

REDHEADED MAN

(*writing as he speaks*) "The wings of the Ulysses Butterfly are iridescent blue-green when fully open and extended..."

GIRL IN ARMCHAIR

Sometimes I wasn't sleeping, sometimes I was just pretending to. I could hear her feet on the carpet outside the door, her hands fingerprinting the windowpanes. Through my half-open eyes, I would see her looking through the glass at me. Her voice sounded oddly far away. She told me about people I didn't know. A boy who flies too close to sun. A man who leaves home only to return twenty years later. A girl who tries to avenge her father's death by killing her mother. Later, she told me he kept books in the trunk of his car. She told me I was too old for this room. She was closing the door and I had to walk away. (*Breath.*) Art was powerful. Or could've been. She told me that too. Art caught her by surprise, left her wanting. She wanted to reach out and touch it.

The man sits up abruptly.

REDHEADED MAN
Where the hell's my eraser?

He flips through the papers on his desk.

GIRL IN ARMCHAIR
Art was everlasting. I learned that one myself. The day I dropped all of her photographs, I picked them up and put them all back where I'd found them, all but one. That first photo that had fallen onto the floor—I slipped you under my shirt when Mom wasn't looking and took you to my room. How old were you then? Twenty-two? Twenty-three? I've never been able to get that picture out of my mind. The way the lines of your body instinctively left one place and entered a new one: the past meet-

ing the present, meeting the future. I didn't care anymore then whether I had a right to touch the photo, claim it as my own. In art class, chalk pastels coated my fingertips with dust. (*Breath.*) Everywhere I went, I left fingerprints.

REDHEADED MAN
It's getting dark. I need a light.

He strikes a match and lights the birthday candle on a frosted cupcake, creating a yellow glow around his work area.

GIRL IN ARMCHAIR
They lived in small glass jars that we kept inside our desks when the final bell rang and we went back home for the evening. I never knew where the second grade teachers got them from exactly. Is there such a thing as mail-order caterpillars? Is there a catalog for these things? There must be. This is what I remember: each day we had to record our observations on worksheets like we were scientists in the middle of an experiment. How fast were the caterpillars growing? How much were they eating? How long had they been alive when they started forming their chrysalis? (*Breath, softly.*) Undergoing their metamorphosis.

REDHEADED MAN
(*whispering*) I'll never finish this.

GIRL IN ARMCHAIR

A metamorphosis. That's what the teachers called it. It wasn't the first time I'd heard the word, but when they said it, it felt different, not at all like the echoes of my mother's voice late at night. The day all the butterflies finally came out, we let them go in the garden we had planted behind our school. It was my eighth birthday that day. In the cafeteria during lunch, I brought everyone cupcakes and they sang "Happy Birthday" before I blew out the candle on my cupcake. That day... (*Breath.*) I wished for the impossible.

The lights on the girl start to dim.

REDHEADED MAN
(*flinches visibly, suddenly*) Shit.

The man reaches around for a tissue and presses it to one of his fingers, then gets up and walks quickly out of the room.

A moment passes.

The girl rises and walks to the desk, closing her book and setting it down in the space where the man had been working.

GIRL IN THE ARMCHAIR
Come back to me.

She blows out the candle.

Black.

Sleep hasn't come easy for me since high school at least, maybe earlier. These days, I like to lie awake in the middle of the night and hold his right hand in mine. It hangs off the side of his mattress tonight, a thick white bandage around the index finger he accidentally sliced open, and with my right hand, I hold his up next to my left to compare. Seems as if I'm always doing this, counting the freckles on both our hands like it's some sort of contest: "who has more?" It's dark. Sometimes I can't see, sometimes I have to guess. Either way, I count until I finally feel my eyes close. I know the afterimage of those freckles, fixed in my mind like burn marks. I lay a grid over it—the lines on the kitchen floor back home playing connect-the-dots, counting. It's a tie. We both win tonight. Or maybe we both lose. Gradually, our freckles fade as the room darkens, leaving the squares of the periodic table drawn to the insides of my eyelids.

I lay my head down on my baby pillow with my left ear pressed up against it, as if I'll still hear something from twenty-three years ago—double doors opening, the future flying past, too fast to remember. Dad's necklace around my neck. The faint sound of sirens outside our window. Beyond them, I can hear Michael breathing.

Three more years of this, and I'll be the same age he was. Some nights I imagine the sand draining slowly from my head: I'm emptying out his dreams.

24

When I read a run-on sentence I'm waiting and searching prematurely for some indication of the end—a resting place of some kind, somewhere to stop and process what I've just taken in. Life is similar in some ways: its constant need for self-referential comments, punctuation in awkward places, a subject cast aside by dependent clauses, the object lost in a sea of prepositions and indefinite articles.

I've stopped trying to hide the fact that I'm no good at puzzles, that I can't always tell the difference between truth and fiction, right and wrong. I've stopped trying to hide the fact that I don't always know what I'm doing.

On the nightstand next to Michael's bed there's an alarm clock and a lamp, a pocket-sized sketchbook, and a Rubik's cube that has never been solved. Until recently, I'd insisted on sleeping on the floor at night, when I slept at all. Of course, we fought about this all the time. "You're being ridiculous," Michael would say. "Who cares if it's my bed, my place?"

I cared because I had stolen things and hidden them under my bed for years. Thinking what? That they could fill some hole in me that only became larger as I dropped my whole world down it? I didn't want to have any secrets from him. "You don't understand," I would say. It was something I said all the time—too often—especially considering that it wasn't true.

Our lives have intersected more than once in the past. Michael knows things about me that he shouldn't know. Exactly how my father said my name the day I was born, for example, said it in a way that transformed future pronunciations into a constant of shuffled syllables—Lyssa somehow reversing and becoming Sally.

I know about the leftover scar near Michael's hip where his mother burned him when he was a toddler.

"Did this hurt?" I ask, with my lips pressed against the crescent shape.

"I don't remember, Lyssa," he says.

"I almost stole your painting once, you know. The one at the restaurant," I say, my voice muffled against his skin. "I was going to walk right off with it." I don't know why I always bring this up when I feel like we're getting too close.

"Will you shut up about that?" he says. "For the last time, I do not care."

Too close again, I think. But to what? To the water in my hair and in my face and me swallowing: the endless stories that come with it.

All of the pillows on the bed smell like his hair—a mixture of sweat and the saltwater sea and some scent I recognize but can never place as belonging to anything organic or natural. I sit up while Michael is still sleeping and examine the Rubik's cube on the table. The red squares are all on one face, but the other colors are still jumbled.

There are boys I once knew who could do it blindfolded or upside down or on a rollercoaster. There are world records for everything.

Michael is different, uninterested in stopwatches and algorithms. I feel the space between him and everything else widen. The evidence of a chasm, the absence of a bridge, present in my skin and on my teeth.

His sketchbooks are always full of blank pages. I flip through them and find some drawings in ballpoint pen, but they always seem to be unfinished.

"It's all up here," he'll say, pointing in the vague direction of his brain, or his ears, or maybe his eyes. "It's best just to get to the real thing, most times. Don't bother with sketches, right?"

I wasn't sure how much I honestly believed that myself. "But, I mean, what if you fuck it up?"

One afternoon—years ago, shortly after we first met—he was sitting at his desk sewing book signatures together. I came up behind him and ran my hand down his chest, then back up again, my arm making a 'V' around his neck.

"You ever want to have kids?" he asked, casually, almost as if my answer was of no consequence.

I left my arm where it was. "What is that supposed to mean?"

"I mean, not with me. Of course."

"Of course." I tapped my cheek with the fingers of my free hand. "Maybe. I was never the kind of girl who sat around planning all that, if that's what you're asking."

There was a rolled up newspaper lying on the floor underneath his desk. Corners of pages were sticking out, everything helter-skelter; I could tell it had already been flipped through. "Are you serious? Have you been reading the obits again?"

He creased this last section of pages he was working on

flat with a bonefolder and added another to the stack, pulling a threaded needle through the first hole. "I don't know what you're talking about. I was just reading up on today's news."

"What do you hope to gain from pretending?" I asked, knowing the answer already, from personal experience, from seeing it so many times before.

And then later, lying in bed with him, half-asleep, I said, "Maybe we can pick up where we left off."

He didn't disagree.

To be honest, he didn't exactly agree either—I got the feeling the whole time we were together that he knew something was odd about our relationship, that every time I looked at him I saw a myriad of other faces. Sometimes one was superimposed on top of the other; other times, one face blended into another so slowly that I could barely tell anything had changed.

"Who am I right now?" he asked me once, afterwards. We were lying side by side, and I turned my head to look at him.

"What?" I didn't know what to say to that, wasn't sure if I'd heard him correctly. Aside from that one night in his studio when he had been preoccupied—trying to finish up a project and meet a tight deadline—I never talked about my parents, or Randy, or my past. I never could remember what exactly I'd said that night either, so what he knew I wasn't quite sure.

"Nothing, it's nothing," he said finally. I knew he wouldn't press the issue.

"Didn't I tell you to stop using these blue bedsheets?" I said, turning away from him, onto my side. "They make me feel like I'm drowning."

The next day, there were fresh sheets on the bed, a dark

tomato red. He never mentioned the conversation again.

Michael told me all the time that I talked in my sleep. I was waiting for it every day when I awoke in the late mornings: "You were talking in your sleep again. Gibberish, I couldn't understand any of it."

Supposedly the only thing I ever said that made any sense was "don't leave me." I said it just like that, "don't leave me," over and over. I never really believed that I'd say something like that—I'm the one who is always leaving.

27

The year I turned seven, my friend Jennah celebrated her birthday in the field behind our elementary school. As tradition dictated, we all ate cupcakes during lunch and then went out to play for recess. Someone had wrapped pieces of white string around all the metal poles and posts across the whole playground structure: on one end of each string was a party favor of some kind—a paint set or a plastic yo-yo maybe—and the other end was where we started, following the string up the ropes and down the monkey bars, wherever it took us. At one central point, a number of different threads intersected, wrapped around the same support beam and I remember getting lost, losing the string amidst all the others that branched away from the beam with it. I grabbed one at random, intuitively, thinking it must be the right one, and followed it to its end: a red sword-shaped pen dangling from one of the play-drive steering wheels.

Thirty seconds later, when I heard another kid crying because there was nothing on the other end of his string, I knew I must have picked the wrong one.

By the time my car pulls up to an empty spot next to the old elementary school, I know I'm going to be late for the reception at the art gallery. But I'm stopping, I'm getting out of the car, I'm slamming the car door. The playground has been rebuilt from

the ground up at least three times since that memory. I trek
through the wet grass as I make my way to the brightly painted
slabs of metal and plastic that form the new structure. At the
bottom of the slides, I start pulling on an imaginary string.

Everything feels strange to me—the playground's individual features shuffled and resting in the wrong places. But I halfway remember the steps I used to take to get where I wanted to
be—two steps forward, four to the right, or something like that.

And with each step, I pull apart words the way my father
did once in his notebooks, pushing them back together in a
new order, with contradictory meanings and reversed syllables.

Endure becomes *end/ure*, becomes *ure/end*, becomes *your
end.*

I sit in front of the steering wheels overlooking the gravel
and pretend to drive away untouched.

I get to the gallery at least half an hour after the reception
has already started. The music playing from the stereo in the
corner is as eclectic as the mix CDs Michael used to play on
a daily basis. "I like this, I want this, send me this," I'd often
said about track six, only to be horrified four minutes later at
track seven: "What the hell are we listening to? Did a cow get
run over by a train and someone just happened to have a tape
recorder at the scene? Turn it off!" Most of the time, he just ig-
nored me, laughed and said to no one in particular, "You should
see your face right now, you really should."

I'm standing in front of the back wall that's been painted
an even black. Near the ceiling, in centered white type are the
words:

FEEL FREE TO TOUCH THE ARTWORK.

The painting that hangs underneath that sentence is the largest one in the gallery tonight. Flames start at the edges of the canvas—a mixture of warm colors applied with long, broad strokes—and blend gradually into a mass of red hair, all the strands working their way towards the center: a young girl's face. And it's a face I'm familiar with, one I might see staring up at me from the kitchen floor after an afternoon of scrubbing her clean. Portraits like these always make me uncomfortable. It's the way she confronts me straight on, her chin up, bone structure defined and exaggerated. The composition defies everything I learned in school: no rule of thirds, no variety in scale and angle. Nothing should be so symmetrical, and I want to look away but don't. In the painting, both her eyes are covered with pairs of butterfly wings, one wing on the left eye, another on the right, blue-green, layers and layers of them, one on top of the other. Somebody has taken a Micron pen and written on the surfaces like they are pages taken out of a book.

I wish I had a magnifying glass to read some of the miniature text. Something about eyes, something about the color blue, something about finally heading home. I think about the house I grew up in and picture myself walking through it backwards, maybe growing young again, through my bedroom and then hers, through his study and around the perimeter of the island counter in the kitchen. The whole while, my mother follows like a silent specter. She's smiling, her eyes darker than I've ever seen them. It's as easy as flipping through a book in reverse. Until, until, until. Back to the beginning, wherever that was. If only I could rip out the pages I'm not so proud of and start over, rewrite those scenes. I'm not afraid to admit that I try.

"Hey, lady, this is an art gallery! What do you think you're doing?" Somebody next to me reaches out for me, tries to stop me.

I want to tell them it doesn't matter. The wings are firmly attached to the canvas. He used magic glue. Of course he did.

The artist himself is near the entrance now, talking to a small group of other artists. I watch his lips from profile as he talks, trying to decipher his words: *I get it, you know. You don't have to explain.* They part briefly and meet again. *Some things are meant to last, some aren't.* Or at least, this is what I'm imagining. I can't actually read lips. His hair has changed slightly since I last saw him, but everything else is still entirely familiar. Maybe I'll walk over later, slide back into conversation with him, the way it once was. But right now he's not facing me, doesn't notice me yet.

I turn my attention back to the wall. To the right of the painting is a small label the size of a business card, fastened onto the wall with silver pushpins:

Icarus and Daedalus, Revisited
Michael Amherst
mixed media on canvas
60 in x 36 in x 2 in

The wings are brittle underneath my fingers, black at the edges, opening and closing as I touch them. This time, they won't fall off and leave, melt by the heat of the fire. I am waving goodbye to the ocean.

ACKNOWLEDGMENTS

Section 1 previously appeared online in *Souvenir Lit* (July 2014)

An excerpt from section 15 previously appeared in the print anthology *The Way We Sleep* (Curbside Splendor 2012)

Section 18 previously appeared online in *elimae* (October 2010)

Section 19 previously appeared online in *Treehouse* (September 2014)

An excerpt from section 23 previously appeared online in *Qu* (Spring 2015)

An excerpt from section 24 previously appeared in *Portland Review* (Spring 2014)

Section 27 previously appeared online in the webzine *I Am: Twenty-Seven* (September 2014)

ABOUT ETCHINGS PRESS

Etchings Press is a student-run publisher at the University of Indianapolis that runs a post-publication award—the Whirling Prize—as well as an annual publication contest for one poetry chapbook, one prose chapbook, and one novella. On occasion, Etchings Press publishes new chapbooks from previous winners. For more information about these contests and the Whirling Prize post-publication award, please visit etchings.uindy.edu.

Previous winners and publications:

Poetry

2022: *A Place That Knows You* by Tiwaladeoluwa Adekunle

2022: *The Vaudeville Horse* by Elizabeth Kerlikowske

2021: *My Mother's Ghost Scrubs the Floor at 2 a.m.*
   by Robert Okaji

2020: *Vaginas Need Air* by Tori Grant Welhouse

2019: *As Lovers Always Do* by Marne Wilson

2018: *In the Herald of Improbable Misfortunes*
   by Robert Campbell

2017: *Uncle Harold's Maxwell House Haggadah* by Danny Caine

2016: *Some Animals* by Kelli Allen

2015: *Velocity of Slugs* by Joey Connelly

2014: *Action at a Distance* by Christopher Petruccelli

Prose

2022: *Triple Point* by Laura Story Johnson (essays)

2021: *Bad Man Love Stories* by Curtis VanDonkelaar (fiction)

2020: *Three in the Morning and You Don't Smoke Anymore* by Peter J. Stavros (fiction)

2019: *Dissenting Opinion from the Committee for the Beatitudes* by Marc J. Sheehan (fiction)

2018: *The Forsaken* by Chad V. Broughman (fiction)

2017: *Unravelings* by Sarah Cheshire (memoir)

2016: *Pathetic* by Shannon McLeod (essays)

2015: *Ologies* by Chelsea Biondolillo (essays)

2014: *Static*: Stories by Frederick Pelzer (fiction)

Novella

2022: *Goodbye to the Ocean* by Susan L. Lin

2021: *Miss Alma May Learns to Fight* by Stuart Rose

2020: *Under Black Leaves* by Doug Ramspeck

2019: *Savonne, Not Vonny* by Robin Lee Lovelace

2018: *Edge of the Known Bus Line* by James R. Gapinski

2017: *The Denialist's Almanac of American Plague and Pestilence* by Christopher Mohar

2016: *Followers* by Adam Fleming Petty

Chapbooks from Previous Winners

2022: *slighted.* by Chad V. Broughman (fiction)

2020: *Fruit Rot* by James R. Gapinski (fiction)

2016: *#LOVESONG* by Chelsea Biondolillo (microessays with photos and found text)

COLOPHON

This book was set in the Calluna font family. The cover text was set in Cambria.

AUTHOR BIOGRAPHY

Susan L. Lin is a Taiwanese American storyteller who holds an MFA in Writing from California College of the Arts. GOODBYE TO THE OCEAN was her undergraduate thesis at the University of Houston. Born in Tennessee and raised in southeast Texas, she currently lives, writes, and sews in southern California. More of her work can be found online at susanllin.wordpress.com.